This Hodder book belongs to:

....

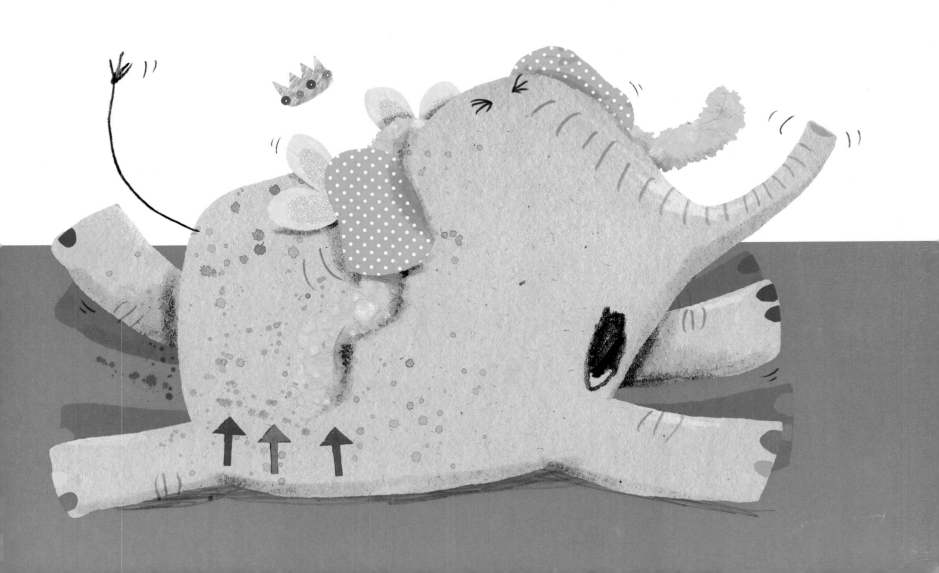

First published in hardback in 2012 by Hodder Children's Books
This edition published in 2018

Text copyright © Gillian Shields 2012
Illustration copyright © Cally Johnson-Isaacs 2012

Hodder Children's Books, Carmelite House
50 Victoria Embankment, London EC4Y 0DZ

ISBN 9781 444 93605 6

Printed in China

Hodder Children's Books is a division
of Hachette Children's Books,
an Hachette UK Company

www.hachette.co.uk

For my darling daughter, my lovely Sasha G.S.
For Dad with love C.J.

Elephantantrum

Gillian Shields and Cally Johnson-Isaacs

Hodder
Children's
Books

A division of Hachette Children's Books

Ellie had **everything.**

But she wanted more. She wanted an elephant.

She wouldn't eat or sleep or brush her hair.
She wouldn't smile or play or do her lessons.
She wouldn't even get out of bed
until she got what she wanted.

'Please get up, Ellie,' said her father.

'NO!' she replied. 'Not until you get me an ELEPHANT!'

Ellie's father went to his big fancy office.

He wrote letters and made phone calls.

He worked and worried and fussed and fretted until…

...an elephant arrived for Ellie.

Ellie jumped up and down in excitement. She couldn't wait to boss her new elephant around.

'Come here, Elephant!' she said.
'Give me a ride! Do a trick!
Pick up my toys!'

The elephant wrapped his trunk around Ellie's waist and lifted her up.

'Ooh!' said Ellie.

'Put me down!'

But the elephant took a good long look at her...

Then he
dropped her
on the floor.
'Ouch!'
said Ellie
furiously.

She had a terrible tantrum.

'I don't want **that** elephant,' she shouted.

'Get me a different one!'

'But it's an extraordinary elephant,' said her father wisely.
'I think it's just the one you need.'

So the elephant stayed and made himself at home.
He slept in Ellie's bed.

He wore her best clothes.

He ate her breakfast.

He played with her toys.

'But they're mine!' Ellie howled.

The elephant took no notice. He even went to school and sat in Ellie's place and played with Ellie's friends.

'Go away!' Ellie ordered.

But the elephant ignored her.

Now the elephant had everything. Ellie even had to make his sandwiches and clean his boots and fold his handkerchiefs. He didn't say 'please' or 'thank you'.

And if Ellie didn't do exactly what he wanted...

eleph

...he had an **enormous**

ntantrum!

Ellie started to cry. The elephant passed
her a handkerchief.

'Thank you,' said Ellie.
It was the first time she had
ever said 'thank you'.

Then Ellie said,
'Please can I have my
things back?'

'Why don't we share them?'
said the elephant.

'All right,' said Ellie happily.
'Let's share.'

So they played together
and it was **brilliant.**

When they went to school, Ellie said,

'Would you **please** give my friends a ride

in the playground?'

'Of course,' said the elephant.

'**Thank you,**' said Ellie.

They all took turns, EVEN Ellie.

It was fun.

It was extraordinary!

That night, Ellie said, 'I hope you'll stay forever.'

'I can't,' said the elephant gently. 'There are other children who need me too. You'll have to share me.'

Ellie didn't scream or shout or have a tantrum. 'I understand,' she said.

And when she woke up, the elephant had gone…

...almost.